I Love You!

Te amo

written by:
Calee M. Lee

illustrated by:
Tricia Tharp

W9-AZC-817

For Audrey and Owen
Text Copyright © Calee M. Lee 2013 Illustration Copyright © Tricia Tharp 2012
All Rights Reserved. No portion of this book may be reproduced without express permission from the publisher.
First Edition
ISBN: 9781623957698
Published in the United States by Xist Publishing
www.xistpublishing.com

Te amo como
  a una piedra saltarina

I love you
    like
      a skipping stone

Te amo como
al hueso de
un perrito

I love you
like
a doggy's bone

Como el mareo que te
da después de rodar
por la colina

Like the dizzy
after rolling down
a hill

Te amo
a una corona
de cumpleaños

I love you
    like
    a birthday crown

Te amo como
   a las plumas de un
        pájaro pequeño

I love you
        like
   a feather's down

Como a una moneda
de suerte
escondida bajo un zapato

Like
a lucky coin
hiding under a shoe

Te amo como
   a la oreja
que escucha un secreto

I love you
like
   a secret's ear

Como a
taza helada con
zarzaparrilla fría

Like

a frosty mug
of cold rootbeer

Como a

un fuerte de almohadas
que se convierte en
una cueva mágica

Like

a pillow fort
that becomes
a magic cave

Te amo como
  a
    una estrella fugaz

I love you
  like
    a shooting star

Por la persona
que eres

For the person
that you are

En el escenario y cuando
nadie te puede ver

On stage and when
no one else can see.

No importa lo
   que hagas a lo a
que le temas

No matter
   what you do or fear

Sabes que
yo estoy siempre cerca

Know that
I am always near

¡Tú eres mi hijo
y
te amo!

You are my child
and
I LOVE YOU!

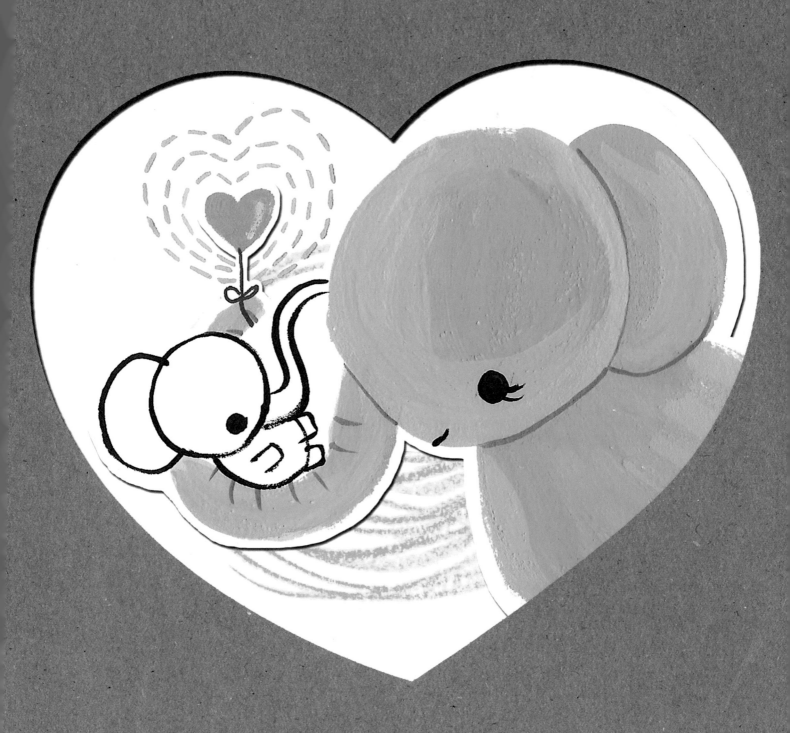

Made in the USA
Lexington, KY
19 July 2018